The Emperor's New Clothes

Illustrated by Val Biro

Award Publications Limited

Once upon a time, there was an emperor who loved fine clothes.

One day two
tricksters came to the
palace to see him.

The men bowed to the Emperor. "We are weavers," they said. "We make the most beautiful cloth, but it is invisible to stupid people."

The Emperor loved fine clothes so much that he had to have some made of the incredible cloth. So he paid the weavers to start work.

The weavers were given a
loom on which to weave their
amazing cloth.

The Emperor sent the Prime Minister to watch them work. But the Prime Minister could not see any cloth on the loom.

Because he did not want the Emperor to think he was stupid, the Prime Minister lied to him.

"The cloth is beautiful!" he exclaimed.

The Emperor was pleased and sent his Head Judge to see the cloth too.

The Head Judge
went to see the cloth. He could
not see it either. But he also did
not want to seem stupid, so he
paid the men with gold coins.

The Head Judge lied
to the Emperor too. "The
cloth is magnificent!" he said.

For weeks the men carefully wove their 'magical' cloth that only clever people could see.

The Emperor heard that people were laughing about the weavers' 'invisible cloth'. He began to worry. What if *he* was stupid and couldn't see it?

The weavers took the magical cloth to show it to the Emperor.

They pretended to cut and sew it to make the Emperor's new clothes.

When they had finished, they asked the Emperor to try them on.

The Emperor could not see the clothes.

But he did not want to seem foolish, so he stood while his 'clothes' were fitted.

"Wonderful!" cried the Head Judge and the Prime Minister.

So the Emperor decided to show off his fine new clothes.

He paraded through the city
and everyone came out to see
the Emperor's new clothes.

People cheered as he went past, but he could hear giggles and whispers too.

As he walked, the Emperor began to wonder if the weavers really were craftsmen, or just crafty?

Perhaps the Prime Minister and Head Judge had only pretended to see the cloth too.

Just then, a small boy stepped forward from the crowd and pointed at him.

"Look, the emperor has no clothes on!"

Everyone stopped
and stared. And then
they started to laugh.

The Emperor blushed. He knew that the boy was right. He now saw that he had been vain and very foolish.